COWS TO THE RESCUE

John Himmelman

Henry Holt and Company

New York

Henry Holt and Company, LLC, *Publishers since 1866*
175 Fifth Avenue, New York, New York 10010 [mackids.com]

Henry Holt® is a registered trademark of Henry Holt and Company, LLC.
Copyright © 2011 by John Himmelman. All rights reserved.

Library of Congress Cataloging-in-Publication Data
Himmelman, John
Cows to the rescue / John Himmelman. — 1st ed.   p.   cm.
Summary: After helping the Greenstalk family get to the county fair, the cows busy themselves finding solutions to many other problems that arise during the day.
ISBN 978-0-8050-9249-3
[1. Cows—Fiction. 2. Agricultural exhibitions—Fiction. 3. Farm life—Fiction. 4. Humorous stories.] I. Title.   PZ7.H5686Co 2011   [E]—dc22   2010036880

First Edition—2011 / Designed by Elizabeth Tardiff / Black Prismacolor pencil for the outline and watercolor paint were used to create the illustrations for this book.
Printed in China by Macmillan Production Asia Ltd., Kowloon Bay, Hong Kong (Vendor Code 10)

7 9 10 8 6

For my editor, Kate—
I couldn't run this farm without you.

It was the day of the county fair!

At seven o'clock, Farmer Greenstalk could not start the car.

Cows to the rescue!

"Thanks for the lift," said Farmer Greenstalk.

At nine o'clock, Jeffrey was sad that he was the only one signed up for the three-legged race.

Cows to the rescue!

"You *all* deserve first place," said Jeffrey.

At eleven o'clock, Ernie the duck got all muddy before the Handsomest Duck Contest.

Cows to the rescue!

"Quack!" said Ernie.

At one o'clock, Mrs. Greenstalk couldn't find her family to pose for funny pictures.

Cows to the rescue!

"These will look great on my refrigerator," said Mrs. Greenstalk.

At three o'clock, Emily wanted to go on the Ferris wheel, but she was too afraid.

Cows to the rescue!

"That wasn't scary at all!" said Emily.

At five o'clock, Jeffrey learned that the pigs hadn't studied for the Smartest Pig Contest.

Cows to the rescue!

"Oink," said the pigs.

At seven o'clock, everyone was exhausted.
Even the cows were too tired to walk all the way home.